To Vida :-)

You are amazing :-)

Sincerely

LUCY and CHESTER'S AMAZING ADVENTURES!

Written by G. Brian Benson

Illustrated by Paul Hernandez

Lucy and Chester's Amazing Adventures!
By G. Brian Benson

Cover design and illustrations by Paul Hernandez

FIRST EDITION

"Be yourself, to free yourself!"

- G. Brian Benson

Just spread your wings and we'll fly far away
To the ends of the earth through night and through day.

We'll sail over mountains and fly above streams

Walk over treetops and float through our dreams.

We'll swim in the ocean with dolphins quite fun

And lie on a beach to dry off in the sun.

Then head to the jungles to play in the trees
With monkeys and parrots amidst a warm breeze.

We'll climb a volcano with lava so thick
We have to turn back at a pace very quick!

Then go to China and hike the Great Wall
As we climb its big stairs feeling quite small.

12

And play the piano in a hall so grand
When I'm through finished playing, they'll all cheer and stand!

Slide down a rainbow and lounge on a cloud
Guided by sunshine so helpful and proud.

Say "hey" to a cowboy riding on by
In a rose colored shirt under blue sky.

Hike in the woods and from rock to rock leap
While playing tag with a kind bighorn sheep.

And fly an old plane with wings colored gold
Doing all kinds of tricks and feeling quite bold.

Then off to the pyramids in Egypt so hot
To have an adventure that could never be bought.

Float down the Nile on our backs all the way
Waving at animals enjoying their day.

And scurry to England to have some fine tea

Then ride a red bus and say hi to the Queen.

21

Explore an old castle with drawbridge and moat
And race through the water in a fine little boat!

Act in a play that would make Shakespeare proud
And then blow kisses to the adoring crowd.

We will then visit Paris at the Eiffel so tall
Looking down at the people who appear very small.

Float on an iceberg in the ocean so vast
Watching a polar bear swim smoothly past.

And then off to Tibet and hope for the chance
To lock eyes with a monk in a knowing glance.

Or ride a large yak on the range so wide
Admiring its beauty with each slow-moving stride.

After Tibet, to a large mountain with snow
And we'll slide and we'll sled shouting, "Go, go, go!"

Having played all day we'll then head for the stars
One final adventure to our special place, Mars.

Spinning around as our heads become light
Circling and speeding in flashes of white.

Then after Mars, we will head home to rest
Lying side by side, to cuddle's the best!

And then wake anew, all rested and spry
To go fly again, new adventures to try!

CPSIA information can be obtained
at www.ICGtesting.com
Printed in the USA
BVHW02*0152100318
510039BV00001B/1/P